SEAMUS McNAMUS

THE GOAT WHO WOULD BE KING

WRITTEN BY **ROB KURTZ**   ILLUSTRATED BY **MIKE LESTER**

SEAMUS McNAMUS

THE GOAT WHO WOULD BE KING

WRITTEN BY ROB KURTZ   ILLUSTRATED BY MIKE LESTER

WORTHWHILE BOOKS

For my royal court: Basia, Sarah, Ariella,
CJ, and Avi, and her Royal Highness,
Queen Elizabeth. — R.K.

To Hope and Grady, who make me proud
that I'm a father. — M.L.

www.myworthwhilebooks.com

ISBN: 978-1-60010-337-7
12 11 10 09 1 2 3 4 5

Seamus McNamus: The Goat Who Would Be King
Text copyright © 2009 Rob Kurtz. Illustrations copyright © 2009 Mike Lester.

Worthwhile Books, a division of Idea and Design Works, LLC. Editorial offices:
5080 Santa Fe Street, San Diego, CA 92109.
Printed in Korea.

Worthwhile Books does not read or accept unsolicited submissions of ideas, stories, or artwork.

Jonas Publishing
Publisher: Howard Jonas

IDW
Chairman: Morris Berger
President: Ted Adams
Senior Graphic Artist: Robbie Robbins

Worthwhile Books
VP & Creative Director: Rob Kurtz
Senior Editor: Megan Bryant
Art Director: Josh White

PRESENT:

Legend has it that long ago in Ireland, a simple farm goat saved his town from an invading army. That's why, to this day, people gather every year at the

Puck Fair

to eat, drink, and be merry. And they always crown a goat to be their king for the three days of the fair.

This is the almost true story of one such goat.

On a pretty little farm in the foothills of Ireland lived
a goat named Seamus McNamus.

Seamus, his wife, Katie, and their son, Billy, made
cashmere wool. Elizabeth and Gertie, the cows, made
milk, and the O'Donnells, a family of chickens, laid eggs.

Life on the farm was simple.

But things were changing. Children who once drank milk were drinking soda instead. Cows can't make soda. Elizabeth and Gertie, being cows, had very little to do.

The wool that goats make for sweaters is beautiful. But sweaters made from nylon cost less. Goats can't make nylon. Seamus, Katie, and Billy, being goats, had very little to do.

And as for eggs—they have too much cholesterol. The O'Donnells, being chickens, didn't know much about cholesterol. But they knew they didn't like it, because they also had very little to do.

No one needed Seamus and his friends anymore.

One day Farmer McFadden decided to have a talk with the animals.

"No one's buying milk, wool, or eggs," he said. "Soon I won't be able to pay my bills.

"When no one wants milk, then a cow is only good for hamburgers," he continued sadly. "If no one wants eggs, then a chicken is just a boneless breast. And a goat, well, I guess in a stew . . ."

The animals did not like what they were hearing. There was panic in the barn!

Clearly Farmer McFadden needed help earning money.
So Seamus decided to get a job. But what could he do? His
skills consisted mostly of making wool and eating flowers.

Elizabeth reminded Seamus that he had recently
eaten Farmer McFadden's calculator. "Maybe you could
be an accountant!" she said.

Billy thought that Seamus could be the flight attendant
who says "Baa-baa" when people leave an airplane.

But Katie thought Seamus should go to the petting zoo to see if they needed a goat.

Seamus didn't want to work in a petting zoo. He wanted to make wool, just like his father and grandfather before him. But his family and friends needed help, so off he went.

As Seamus walked to the zoo, suddenly he heard the sound of trumpets and horns ring through the air. A voice called, "Let the Puck Fair begin!"

People ran from the town, shouting, "Find the king! Find the king!"

How could they lose the king? Seamus wondered.

A moment later, a boy threw a rope around Seamus.
Seamus screamed, "Aaaaahhh!"
But, unfortunately, it came out sounding like "Baaaa!"
"I found the king!" the boy yelled.
Me? thought Seamus. *The king? Are you crazy?*
I'm a goat.

Seamus pleaded with the boy, "Listen, I'm not
the king! I'm a goat hoping to get a job at the petting zoo."
But, unfortunately, it came out sounding like "Baaaa."

An eager crowd of people surrounded Seamus, cheering, "Hooray for our king!" Then a big burly man picked up Seamus and offered him a barrel of pickles.

Seamus loved pickles.

Seamus decided he'd try being king for a little while, at least until he finished all the pickles.

Before long, Seamus forgot all about the troubles on the farm. He was having a great time eating and dancing. Seamus loved being king!

And then it happened. Seamus got sick from eating too many pickles. He needed his bed.

Seamus left the fair after dark, so no one noticed that the king was gone. But the long walk home, with a belly full of pickles, was not easy.

When Seamus got home, he told everyone about his day as king. The animals were amazed.

Then Katie said, "Wait a second! You were the king and all you did was eat pickles and have fun?"

No one was happy with Seamus.

The next morning Katie woke Seamus early and said, "Farmer McFadden needs money. Go back to the fair and get him some!"

Seamus wasn't sure how to make enough money to save the farm.

Then he had an idea.

Word quickly spread at the fair that the goat who was king was also a great dancer!

Soon people crowded around to see their king dance. They clapped and cheered and threw money—lots and lots of money!

When Seamus got home, he sheepishly told the animals what had happened. "What are we going to do?" they cried. "You're king for only one more day!"

Gertie looked out the window and saw Farmer McFadden sharpening his knives. "We're goners," she said with a sigh.

"Wait! I have an idea!" Seamus exclaimed. "What if people needed us again?"

"Us?" Elizabeth asked. "Nobody needs us."

Seamus danced onto the stage, showing off a
beautiful homemade Irish sweater.
And everyone *oooh*ed and *ahhh*ed.

Next, Seamus cooked an egg and smothered it with ketchup, because that's how Seamus liked his eggs.

And everyone *oooh*ed and *ahhh*ed.

Then Seamus grabbed a bottle of milk and drank it all in one gulp!

And everyone *oooh*ed and *ahhh*ed.

Finally, Seamus pointed to the curtain behind him. The crowd leaned forward to see what it was hiding.

Seamus lifted the curtain to reveal the animals, who
were eager to show everyone what they had to offer.

The crowd roared with delight and came running over to buy milk, eggs, and sweaters.

Then Seamus remembered that this was his last day as king. Soon he would be just a goat again. Seamus knew what he wanted his final kingly act to be. So he stood on his throne and issued a royal proclamation:

By Order of the King

Now and forever, people throughout the land shall enjoy eggs, milk, and homemade sweaters.

But all the pickles belong to the king!

But, unfortunately,
it came out sounding like,

"Baaa,

baaa,

baaa!"